Purchased for
Citizens for Life,
a grant provided by the
California State Library/
California Civil Liberties
Public Education Program
through the Stockton-
San Joaquin County
Public Library
and the Japanese
American Citizens
League of Stockton

So far from the Sea

By **Eve Bunting**   Illustrated by **Chris K. Soentpiet**

Clarion Books/*New York*

$\mathcal{M}$y mom and dad, my
little brother Thomas, and I
have been driving since early
morning. It's afternoon now.
We've driven along this road
before, and I know we're almost
there. Thomas knows, too, and
he's quiet, watching.

In the distance, on both
sides, are dark snow-topped
mountains, dull as the February
sky. The road is straight and
endless. Crows strut in the
stubbly fields. Does Thomas
feel spooky and scared the way
I do? Maybe he is too
little to understand.

"Here it is," Dad says, and
I see the two rough wooden
planks sticking out of the dirt
at the side of the road. We pull
into the space beside them.

Dad says there was once a sign that hung between those wooden planks. MANZANAR WAR RELOCATION CENTER, it said. Once there was a barbed wire fence, so you couldn't get in or out of the place without permission. Once there were guard towers with searchlights on top. The towers are gone now, along with almost everything else.

Farther back from the road, I can see the small stone gatehouse with its boarded-up window and strange pointed roof. That gatehouse is one of the few things left. We've driven to Manzanar four times and I remember every one of them. I should be used to this place, but I'm not. I shouldn't be nervous, but I am.

"Laura! Thomas! Put on your jackets and boots," Mom tells us. We've taken them off in the nice, steamy warmth of the car, but now we struggle back into them. I check my right-hand pocket. The folded neckerchief is still there.

"Make sure you have your gloves," Mom reminds us.

Dad opens the door and an icy wind from the Sierra whooshes into the car.

Thomas squinches back. "Can't we drive to where Grandfather is?"

Dad shakes his head. "This will probably be the last time we come here. I want us to walk through the camp."

It will probably be the last time because we are moving from California to Boston, Massachusetts. That's very far away. There's a sea in Boston, too, and Dad says we can see it from our new house. I think how much Grandfather would have liked that. To him, the sea was everything. I can't bear to think we have to leave him here.

Dad opens the trunk and Mom takes out the beautiful silk flowers we made to bring with us. The other times we came, we brought real flowers, but we know they probably died fast and blew away. Bringing silk ones today was Mom's idea.

We start walking across the wide dirt field. It is huge, bigger than the most enormous football field, and there's nothing on it but a few scrubby trees and bent-over shrubs. It's hard to imagine that once thousands of people lived here, and there were barracks and a hospital and churches and a school where my dad went. The way it was almost seems like a picture on a blackboard that got wiped out by a giant eraser.

We walk side by side, the four of us. Tire tracks wiggle around us in the soft dirt. There have been people here before us, people who came and left again.

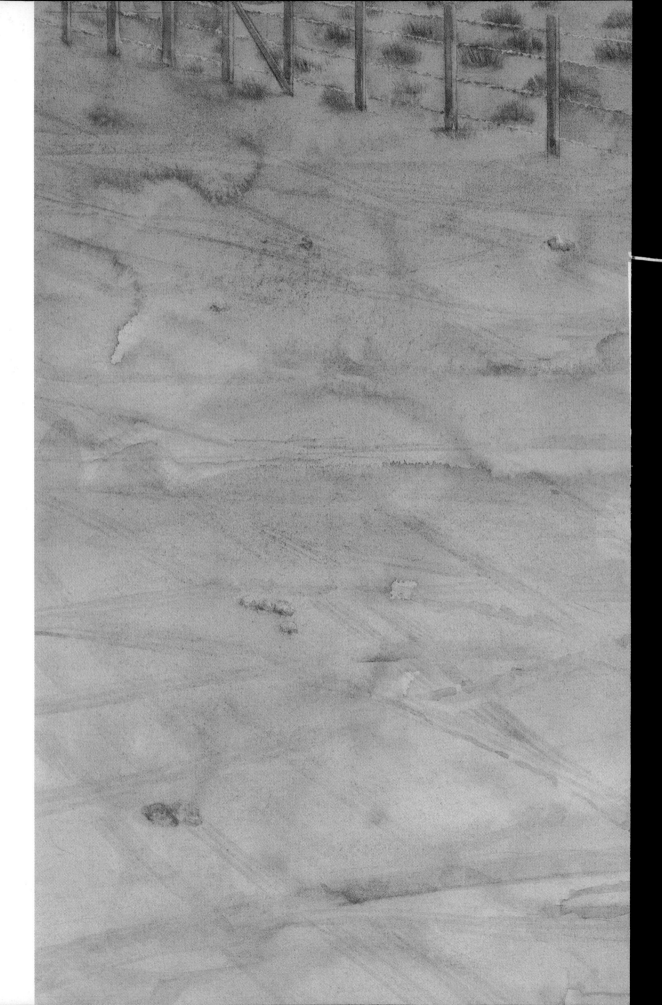

My dad is smiling down at me. "There was a song we used to sing when we were in this camp. It was popular in 1942." Dad has a terrible voice but he sings anyway, quietly. Manzanar is a quiet kind of place.

"Give me land, lots of land, under starry skies above.

Don't fence me in."

He shakes his head. "Can you imagine? We were just kids. I'm not sure we even thought what those words meant."

Part of an old faucet is sticking out of the dirt. Thomas falls over it.

Thomas would.

"Let's keep going, pal," Dad says, and Thomas limps on. I see he is holding Mom's hand. Thomas doesn't like to hold anyone's hand. He must feel the scariness of this awful place, too.

"Why did they put you and Grandmother and the aunts and uncles here, anyway?" he asks.

Dad pulls his head far back in his hood, like a snail going into its shell. "Because Japan attacked the United States," he says. "It was a terrible thing. Suddenly we were at war. And we were Japanese, living in California. The government thought we might do something to help Japan. So they kept us in these camps."

Dad has explained this a hundred times, but Thomas forgets because he is so little.

"It wasn't fair," I say. "It was the meanest thing in the whole world. You were Americans. Like I am. Like Thomas."

Dad shrugs. "It wasn't fair that Japan attacked this country either. That was mean, too. There was a lot of anger then. A lot of fear. But it was more than thirty years ago, Laurie. We have to put it behind us and move on."

He looks toward the mountains. "I used to watch those. They'd change with every season. In summer, at sunset, they were pink and a shadow like a giant eagle would fall across them. I'd wish I could climb on its back and fly away . . . far, far, away."

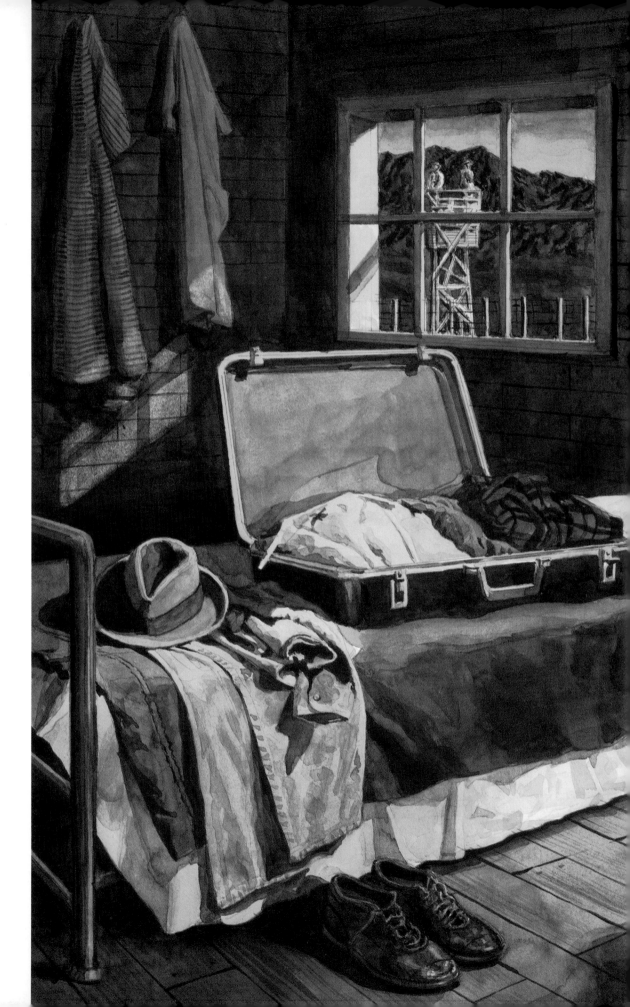

I stare at the mountains, trying to imagine my dad then. He was eight years old, a year older than I am, three years older than Thomas.

We stop while Thomas pulls up his socks. They always slide down inside his boots. It's bad to stop, though. When there's no sound of our footsteps crunching the dirt, I can feel the ghosts watching us, the ghosts of the ten thousand people who once lived here. I hear them whispering.

"Was your camp better than this one?" I ask Mom, speaking so there'll be a real sound. Way back then she was in a camp, too.

She lifts the silk flowers and smells them, though they have no smell. "It was colder in Wyoming, where I was," she says. "The snow was deeper."

The wind is gusting, blowing ice prickles on my face. Mom's flowers rustle. I see a piece of twisted tree root on the ground and pick it up. This will be perfect.

"Look! Look! There's the monument," Thomas says, running ahead.

The monument is tall and thin and white. An obelisk, Dad calls it. It looks so weird standing out here in the middle of nothingness. On it, in black Japanese script, are the words MEMORIAL TO THE DEAD. It marks the cemetery that lies behind a wire fence.

We go in through an opening.

People have left offerings at the monument, held down by pieces of wood or stones. There are origami birds, their wings trapped under little rocks. A broken cup holds crumbs of a rice cake. There are bits of colored glass, some coins. A bare cherry tree branch is stuck inside one of the cracks in the base.

I turn my head and see my grandfather's grave among the others circled round with stones. He died in this camp. The doctors said it was from pneumonia, but my father says Grandfather began dying the day the soldiers came for them, to put them in buses and bring them here.

Grandfather was a tuna fisherman. He had his own boat, *Arigato*, which means "thank you" in Japanese. He was always thankful for his good life. My father never found out afterward what happened to the boat or to Grandmother and Grandfather's house. He said the government took those things and Grandfather's dignity along with them when they brought him here, so far from the sea.

Dad told me that while Grandfather was in the camp he went out every morning to check the sky and the clouds and smell the weather. "A good day for fishing," he'd say.

Instead of a headstone, Grandfather has rocks piled one on top of the other like a small tower. His name, Shiro Iwasaki, and the date, 1943, are painted on the top stone.

Dad lifts away a tumbleweed that has blown inside the circle of rocks around the grave. Mom lays the flowers where the tumbleweed was, and Dad weighs their stems down with a heavy rock. We stand, looking at the purple and yellow and scarlet silk flowers against the brown dirt. Wind moves the petals.

"I'm cold," Thomas says, jumping up and down.

"We can go now," Dad says.

"Wait." I take a small, folded piece of cloth from my pocket.

"What is it?" Dad looks closer. "It's my old Cub Scout neckerchief," he says, and turns to Mom. "I thought my uniform went to the Goodwill with the rest of the stuff."

"I took the scarf out of the bag," I say. "I wanted to bring it to Grandfather."

Dad looks at me for a moment, then nods.

I shake out the folds, put the faded yellow neckerchief in front of the stone tower where Grandfather's name is painted, and hold it in place with the tree root.

"But why is Laura *doing* this?" Thomas asks. "It's not Grandfather's."

"Because I told her a story once." Dad's voice comes from some remembering place. "When they came for us, my father said to me, 'Koharu! Put on your Cub Scout uniform. That way they will know you are a true American and they will not take you.' I put it on. But they took me anyway. They took all of us."

"I brought the scarf to Grandfather because he was a true American," I say.

Dad nods. "Thank you, Laura."

Dark clouds pile around the mountaintops. Night is coming. We huddle close.

"We should leave," Mom says.

Dad holds her arm as we walk.

"It was wrong," I whisper. "Wrong. Wrong."

"Sometimes in the end there is no right or wrong," Dad says. "It is just a thing that happened long years ago. A thing that cannot be changed."

We stop while Thomas pulls up his socks. I look back. I never knew my grandfather, but I love him and I don't want to leave him here.

The two ends of the neckerchief have come loose and flutter free. I can see the top of the tree root. It looks like a boat—a boat with sails skimming the wind, heading away from this unhappy place.

A boat, moving on.

Afterword

In 1942, two months after the Japanese bombed United States warships at Pearl Harbor, President Franklin D. Roosevelt signed Executive Order 9066. It stated that all people of Japanese ancestry living on the West Coast of the United States must be placed in relocation camps. Many of those interned were American citizens.

Manzanar, in eastern California, was the first of ten War Relocation Centers. It had a population of approximately ten thousand.

In this story, it is 1972 and the Iwasakis go back to visit the camp where the father was interned for three and a half years. The Iwasaki family is fictional, but there are thousands of American citizens of Japanese ancestry with the same kinds of memories.

Manzanar was closed in 1945 and its buildings were sold at auction. The area where the camp stood is now a National Historic Site. The small cemetery is still there.

For Mr. Ron Janson, who gave me my own corner studio at Grant High.
Bless you for your generosity and faith in me.—C.K.S.

Clarion Books • a Houghton Mifflin Company imprint • 215 Park Avenue South, New York, NY 10003 • Text copyright © 1998 by Eve Bunting • Illustrations copyright © 1998 by Chris K. Soentpiet • The illustrations for this book were executed in watercolor. • The text is set in 16/20-point Caslon. • All rights reserved. • For information about permission to reproduce selections from this book, write to Permissions, Houghton Mifflin Company, 215 Park Avenue South, New York, NY 10003. • Printed in the USA. • "Don't Fence Me In" (Cole Porter) ©1944 (Renewed) Warner Bros. Inc. All rights reserved. Used by permission.

• LIBRARY OF CONGRESS CATALOGING-IN-PUBLICATION DATA •

Bunting, Eve, 1928-   So far from the sea / by Eve Bunting ; illustrated by Chris K. Soentpiet.   p.   cm.   Summary: When seven-year-old Laura and her family visit Grandfather's grave at the Manzanar War Relocation Center, the Japanese American child leaves behind a special symbol.   ISBN 0-395-72095-8   1. Japanese Americans–Juvenile fiction. [1. Japanese Americans–Fiction. 2. Manzanar War Relocation Center–Fiction. 3. Grandfathers–Fiction.]   I. Soentpiet, Chris K., ill.   II. Title.   PZ7.B91527Slh 1998   [E]–dc21   97-28176   CIP   AC

HOR 10 9 8 7 6 5 4 3 2